D0460764

Full Moon
Monster Madness

pi
kids®

publications international, ltd.

No one has been in the old Witherspoon place in 75 years. Folks round here say it's haunted. I say there's no such thing as ghosts. Let's spend the night and find out! First find me, Brave Dave. Then look for my friends.

Brave Dave

Faint-hearted Faye

Horrified Horace

Nervous Nellie

Frightened Fred

Shaky Jake

Trembling Trudy

Chilly Willy

Hildegard checked her broom at the door and entered the giant hall. This was the 13th Annual Witch Convention, and it promised to be the best show ever!

First find Hildegard. Then look for these great new witch products.

Hildegard

Kleer-Vu Crystal-Ball Cleaner

BAT WING HELPER

Bat-Wing Helper

Turbo broom

Saf-T-Helmet

Self-stir cauldron

SPELZ

Spell book

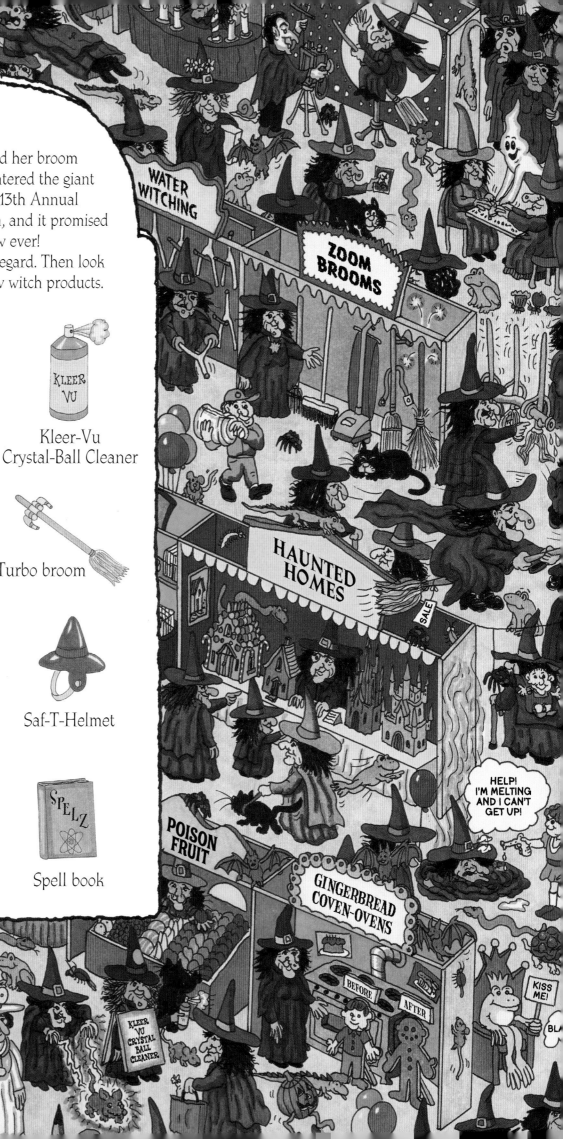

No bones about it: Shady Acres Cemetery is one crazy joint tonight! The place is shakin'! Everyone who is anyone is there.

Don't be a deadbeat—see if you can find these Very Important Skeletons!

Sherlock Holmes

King Tut

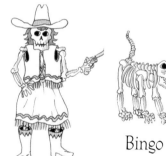

Annie Oakley

Bingo

Anne Boleyn

Long John Silver

Genghis Khan

Some beastly noises were coming from Dr. Frankenstein's laboratory. The mad scientist burst into the room. "It's a zoo in here!" he cried. And it was. An electrical storm had given life to all of his experiments.

First find the doctor. Then see if you can find all of these custom-made creatures.

Dr. Frankenstein

A pigosaurus

A sheepigator

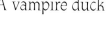

A vampire duck

A bearephant

A cock-a-poodle-doo

A squish

DADDY
GENERAL LEE SHOCKING

MUMMY

BAD FIRE   GOOD FIRE

CIGARS

20 V

QUIT WHILE YOU'RE A HEAD

SPARE PARTS

Boo, pardner! Welcome to Deadman's Gulch, a real *live* Western ghost town. The place has been deserted for 100 years. Too bad the citizens don't know it! Take a look around. Can you find these ghostly Western things?

A ghostly cactus

A ghostly warrior

A ghostly bandit

A ghostly sheriff

A ghostly coyote

A ghostly stagecoach

A ghostly rattlesnake

WELCOME

FISHIN HOLE

SPECIFIC STORE

SALOON

SALOON

THE DUSTY GULLET

GOOD CENTS BANK

GHOST TOWN TOURS

So! You think you can withstand torture? Then you have never been to the Chamber of 1,001 Horrors! You may choose your torture. Can you find these all-time favorite devices?

Home movies

Being tickled

Going to the dentist

Doing push-ups

Eating spinach

Washing dishes

Kissing Aunt Agnes

Long division

WELCOME TO THE CHAMBER OF 1,001 HORRORS HAVE A NICE DAY!

Pete's Pumpkin Patch sure gets busy round this time of year. Folks come from miles around for hayrides, apple dunkin', and pumpkin pickin'.

Some of Pete's employees are *outstanding* in their field. Can you find them?

Corncob Bob

Sweet Sally

Flour-sack Jack

Punkinhead Patty

Apple Betty

Raggedy Annie

Haywood W. Haystack, III

Johnny Potts

PONY RIDES

PIE EATING CONTEST

PUMPKIN ICE CREAM

PUMPKIN JUICE

PUMPKIN LANE

PUMPKIN
PIES, CAKES, BREAD, SOUP, CANDY, DONUTS, PANCAKES, PIZZA, PUDDING, COOKIES

GUESS HOW MANY SEEDS

The Transylvania High School Spring Prom was a costume ball this year. The band played until the sun came up, and all the costumes were monstrously good. Some monsters looked real — because they were! Can you find these real monsters partying with the other prom-goers?

A space alien

A gill man

An ogre

A werewolf

A mummy

A vampire

Frankenstein's monster

A blob

YOU'RE IN VAMPIRE COUNTRY GO COUNTS!

CHICKEN SOUP

The Smith family packed a picnic and went to the park for the day. How could they know what horrors awaited them? The Goblin family was having its annual reunion!

There was a lot of weird food at the park that day. Can you find these things the picnickers were gobblin'?

Goblin noodle soup

Goblin chips

Goblin à la mode

Goblinade

Goblin sandwich

Goblin salad

Fried goblin

The ghosts in the haunted house were good sports about their uninvited guests. Can you find ghosts playing these sports?

★ Basketball
★ Roller-skating
★ Baseball
★ Golf
★ Billiards
★ Football
★ Table tennis
★ Bowling
★ Skiing

Many witches brought their pets to the convention. Can you find them?

★ Thirteen black cats
★ Thirteen warty toads
★ Thirteen green lizards
★ Thirteen poisonous snakes
★ Thirteen fat rats
★ Thirteen bats
★ Thirteen black widow spiders

Go back to Shady Acres Cemetery — if you dare. Can you find these "dead" things?

★ A dead end
★ A dead ringer
★ A doornail
★ A dead lift
★ A death blow
★ "At death's door"
★ Dead weight

Mixed up in the mess that was once Dr. Frankenstein's lab, there are some unaltered animals. Can you find them?

★ A tabby cat
★ An ostrich
★ A Dalmatian
★ A goldfish
★ A skunk
★ A monkey
★ A frog
★ A bull